OFF THE
TRACK

The creators of this book recognise and acknowledge the traditional custodians of the land through which the Bibbulmun Track passes.

For Deepika, the Harrys
and adventurous families everywhere

OFF THE TRACK

CRISTY BURNE

ILLUSTRATED BY AMANDA BURNETT

FREMANTLE PRESS

ALL UNPACKED

Harry had just finished packing his bag when Deepika's mum unzipped it and took everything out again. She started a pile of his things, right there, on the floor of his new apartment.

'You won't be needing this on the track,' she told him. 'Or these. Or this.' His best spinner. His trading cards. His remote-controlled car. They all went on the pile. Then, after she'd taken everything fun out of his bag, she stood there, holding out her hand.

'What?' he said, pretending not to know.

'Come on,' she said. 'Your phone.'

Now he pretended not to hear. 'What?'

'You won't need a phone. We'll be embracing

the great outdoors. It'll be our time to get to know each other.'

She beamed at him. Harry's eyes grew wide. They'd only just met, but he already knew all he wanted to know about Deepika's mum. Ana was bossy. She dressed like a farmer. And she was obviously deranged. 'No way, I need it.' He held his phone close and looked for his mum. She knew about phones. She'd save him.

But Mum was in the other room, on her phone.

He thought Deepika would surely understand. She was a kid. But when he looked to her for help she just smiled at him. She didn't even seem to realise her mum was being a fruit loop. Or perhaps she was used to this behaviour.

'There won't be much reception out there anyway,' said Ana, still holding out her hand.

Harry wanted to back away. Or run. Or hide.

'It'll just be extra weight to carry,' Ana pushed on. 'You really won't need a phone.'

Now Harry did take a step back. 'But I really will', he insisted.

But Ana didn't seem to hear. 'Just leave it on the pile', she said, and started folding a T-shirt. 'Do you have a rain jacket? What about an extra jumper?'

This was brutality. 'I'm entitled to my freedom'. Harry puffed out his chest. 'And my basic human rights'. Without a phone there'd be Nothing To Do. And he was pretty sure Not Dying Of Boredom was a human right.

'Exactly', said Ana, still sorting his belongings. 'Deepika, can you get Harry a spare spare-jumper? There's a pile on the couch'.

'Okay', chimed Deepika. She turned to Harry with another enormous smile. 'I'll lend you my favourite', she said, and skipped away.

Just then Mum returned from her phone call. Harry could've kissed her.

'Mum, I can bring my phone on the hike, can't I? I'll take care of it and I won't stay up late, plus you

know how annoying I can be when I'm bored …'

He tried to flutter his eyelashes, but Mum was looking to Ana instead. Unbelievable. Mum hadn't seen Ana in twenty years, but now, just because they were back in the same city, they were acting like long-lost sisters. Worse, even though Harry and Deepika had only just laid eyes on each other, suddenly, just because their mums were old friends, they were supposed to be all buddy-buddy best friends forever, too. Ugh.

And way worse than all that put together, the absolute worst, in fact, was that this was only the beginning. Mum had dragged Harry all the way from Sydney. And they were here to stay. He'd had to say goodbye to all his friends. His school. Their old apartment. The only life he'd ever known — and it had been a good life, too.

And now this.

'Here,' said Deepika, holding out a brandless blue jacket he wouldn't wear even if he was alone and freezing in Antarctica and it was snowing. 'It's so soft, feel it.'

'Don't forget repellent,' Ana said to Mum. 'The horseflies can really bite.'

'And it's so warm,' said Deepika. She pushed the jacket at him. 'Feel it. That's why I love it so much.'

This had to be some sort of demented dream. Harry looked pleadingly at Mum. Surely she could see? This whole move had been a horrible mistake. And spending an entire weekend tramping around stinking-hot, snake-filled scrub with only lunatics for company was another horrible mistake. If she was really so desperate for a long-lost Ana-reunion, why couldn't they re-une at a resort? Somewhere with a pool, and a flat-screen and a DVD collection.

Harry appealed with his eyes. 'Mum, I seriously need my phone.'

Mum looked at Ana again and Ana just shrugged. 'It's your choice Charl, but there won't be much need for phones. As long as we have one for emergencies.' She returned to matching socks.

Mum nodded with relief. 'Right, okay.' She slipped her own phone into her jacket pocket and shrugged apologetically at Harry. 'Sorry mate. We only need one.'

Unbelievable. 'But Mum!'

'Surely you can leave it at home, just for a weekend,' she said, but she couldn't meet his eye. That's because she knew full well what she was asking. Mum would have a nervous breakdown if she ever had to leave her phone for just five minutes, let alone an entire weekend.

'Here,' said Deepika. 'You can borrow these socks. They're like walking on pillows.'

'Does everyone have sunscreen?' Ana asked.

'Mum …' appealed Harry.

But she was gone, into the other room to make one last call.

And so just like that, the decision was made. No

phone. One whole wasted weekend. Unbelievable.

Later, piled into the back seat of Ana's car with Deepika, Harry slouched as low as his seatbelt would go, and scowled.

In the front passenger seat, Mum was using her phone to check the maps app. Which was totally unfair, and she knew it. 'Look Harry,' she said, all forced cheer and fake smile. She reached round to show him her screen. 'Not long now.'

She was obviously feeling guilty. Well, good. He was glad, and he scowled some more.

'Bye-bye civilisation,' cheered Ana. 'Bring on the bush!'

'Yay!' cheered Deepika.

Ugh, thought Harry.

ON THE TRACK

An hour later and they hadn't walked a single step.
Harry was exhausted. He was stuck, still, with
Deepika in the back of Ana's car. Their mothers
were chatting non-stop about jobs and schools
and old friends and other jobs. And whenever
they paused so Mum could check messages on her
phone, Deepika would jump in and never stop.

'Camping is awesome and hiking is even
better and I can't wait to eat hot noodles and toast
marshmallows and jump over logs and this one
time we climbed a tree, and I could see across the
whole forest, and when the wind blew you could
feel the whole tree move, but I wasn't scared even

though it was really, really high.' She paused for breath, then leaned closer. 'Well, a bit scared.' She grinned a huge grin at him. She seemed to do that a lot. 'Have you ever climbed a really, really high tree?'

Harry just shrugged. His old apartment was really, really high, if that counted. But he hadn't had much call for tree climbing.

'Well, have you been hiking?' Deepika persisted.

Harry shrugged.

'Well, what about camping?'

He shrugged again. He didn't want to make friends with Deepika. He was more into proper-fun things, like gaming and Netflix. Not camping and pillow socks.

Hours later, right when vital parts of Harry were turning numb, Ana pulled into what she referred to as the car park. It was actually an abandoned sand patch, ringed by miles of deserted scrub.

Mum lasted approximately twelve seconds before she confirmed that her phone had no reception. Then she started having some sort of semi-cyborg meltdown.

'But I didn't realise …' she spluttered. 'What about my messages …? What about work?' She stared desperately around her, into the sand, into the bush, as if willing a phone tower to somehow rise from the undergrowth.

Ha! thought Harry. Serves you right.

And then Mum shrieked. 'What's that?'

Harry spotted a dusty red sedan, hidden further down the dirt road and a few metres into the bush. He knew what it was immediately. A stolen car. And the driver was probably on the run from the police. With a fistful of diamonds. Also stolen. Probably from a celebrity. Offering an enormous cash reward for their return. He saw it on his newsfeed all the time.

'Should we call the police?' Mum asked.

But Ana had obviously never lived in Sydney. 'It'll belong to another hiker. Some people prefer to hide their car than use the car park,' she said, giving Mum a reassuring pat on the shoulder. 'Just don't leave anything valuable on display. Now, who needs a hand with their pack?'

Unbelievable.

Ana heaved her backpack up onto her shoulders. She looked like some sort of travelling circus, with plastic mugs and dirty thongs and blackened pots and water bottles all hanging off her. And they were only going for one night.

Harry looked across at Deepika. Okay, so she was odd, but surely another kid would understand about stolen diamonds. He wondered about asking her, except she didn't seem to care, perhaps not even about the cash reward. She was tightroping along a log. Her dark hair hung in one shiny plait down the middle of her backpack, and she was wearing a collared shirt, quick-dry trousers and sturdy-looking shoes.

Harry was wearing his new sneakers and a gaming T-shirt. He'd wanted to wear jeans but Boss of All Things Ana had said no. So now he was stuck with board shorts. He wondered about tightroping on the log, but it didn't look all that fun really.

Deepika caught him watching and grinned. 'How heavy's your pack? Mine's mega-heavy. I'm even carrying my own sleeping bag. Mum finally let me. Plus I've got snakes, and smarties, and chocolate frogs, and a whole packet of chips. I love chips. And a spare jumper.' She grinned even wider. 'Of course, a spare jumper. How 'bout you?'

Harry blinked. His pack was his schoolbag, not a proper pack, and it was still in the boot of the car.

'Did you bring much chocolate?' Deepika asked.

Harry sighed loudly and pulled his bag from the boot. It was surprisingly light, but he wasn't telling Deepika that. It was Ana's fault anyway. She'd had taken out all the heavy stuff.

Ana helped Mum put on her pack. It was Ana's old one, big and faded blue and stuffed to the brim. He really couldn't believe Mum was doing this. Neither of them liked being outdoors. Mum must've been distracted by her phone when Ana had invited them. She'd agree to a lot when she was texting.

'All ready?' Ana asked.

'Ready!' Deepika chimed, still super-cheery, which seemed to be her only mode.

Ana did some last-minute checks and locked the car. Mum made them all pose near the track sign while she took a million photos. With her phone. Harry made sure he looked wounded in every shot.

'I can't get online,' Mum said, 'but I'll post them as soon as I can.' Her voice only broke a little and Harry was reluctantly impressed. She'd existed almost fifteen minutes with no reception. It had to be a new record.

'Let's get moving!' Ana announced.

Deepika whooped and then jumped the first few metres along the dirt path. Literally. Her giant plait bounced with each bound.

Harry walked. Carefully. He'd googled about surviving in the bush. There were wild pigs with gigantic goring tusks. Plus snakes, real ones, with deadly poisonous fangs. And ticks, with about a million spindly legs and blood-sucking jaws. And mosquitoes, the kind that carry strange tropical diseases and make you itch till your leg goes bright red and then explodes. Although he might have made up the exploding part.

And right now there were trees with blackened trunks stretching away on either side. Scrub with dagger-sized thorns crowding in. Giant ants with sharpened pincers all over the track. Plus glistening spider webs, and probably even spiders. The kind that pierce you with dripping fangs to inject paralysing venom. You'd be dead in minutes. Or was that hours? Harry wasn't sure which was worse.

And no one really knew what lay ahead. You could walk for months on this track and still not reach the end. Even Ana had never walked this stretch before. She said that was part of the adventure. Unbelievable.

'You want to go first?' Deepika asked.

Harry gulped.

Deepika waved him forward. 'Go on. Being the leader is way fun.'

Ana waited. Mum did too. Flies buzzed and crickets or frogs or some sort of noisy chirping creature chirped. Crows cawed in the distance.

'Nah, you go,' he said.

Deepika stepped past him, leading them out and along the track.

Harry had been walking for around four seconds when Ana called out: 'You sure that's the right way?'

Ugh. Lost already. Had Ana set them up on purpose? Harry turned, but Ana was smiling.

'Well done,' she said. 'Our first Waugal.'

She was talking to Deepika, who was pointing at a tree. And incredibly, perhaps for the first time since they'd met, Deepika was silent. Not so incredibly, she was beaming.

'What's a Waugal?' asked Mum.

'The snake,' said Ana.

'What!?' said Mum. 'Where!?'

Harry looked everywhere for a snake, then noticed Ana trying not to laugh. 'There.' She pointed to Deepika's tree.

Tacked into the tree's lined trunk was a yellow triangle about the size of Harry's fist. On the triangle was a picture of a twisting black and yellow snake.

'That's our trail marker,' Ana explained. 'A picture of the Rainbow Serpent. In Noongar culture, the Waugal is the giver of life, and it shaped this land. Stick with the Waugal and it'll take us where we need to be.'

I need to be in Sydney, thought Harry. Preferably on the couch. I bet it can't take me there.

'Oh,' said Mum. 'Nice.' She pulled out her phone and took a photo of the trail marker. Then another.

'So,' said Ana. 'Which way do we go?'

Harry half-shrugged. The yellow triangle was shaped like an arrowhead, and it was pointing the same way they were walking. So he half-pointed in that direction.

'Nice one,' smiled Ana.

Deepika gave Harry a thumbs-up, then she turned and kept walking. In the same direction they'd been going before. Harry wondered if the day could get any more tedious. Then, after thirty more seconds, Mum called out.

'Wait a sec, I have to grab a picture of this view,' she said, pulling out her phone. Harry sighed. It would be a great shot, and if he'd had his phone he would've taken a photo too. Instead he tried hard to look like a disadvantaged artist. Hopefully Mum would see him and feel terrible.

But if Mum did see, she didn't seem to care. Instead, she seemed to be doing her best to enjoy the trip, despite the no-reception thing. Perhaps she was more used to the outdoors than Harry gave her credit for. He remembered once she'd had a pot plant on their balcony.

'Let's go!' urged Deepika.

Soon they had walked non-stop for two whole minutes, which Harry decided was long enough to see all there was to see. Scrub. Sand. Sky. Done.

Except then they walked some more. And more. And more. And more and more and more. Ahead of him, Deepika chattered and chattered. And chattered and chattered and chattered. She seemed happy about everything.

'Oh, this is cool, just watch out for snakes,' she

said, clambering over a fallen log. 'Real snakes, I mean.'

Harry watched, closely, trying not to puff.

'Check this out, which way will you go? I'm going left,' she said, winding around a hollow stump.

Harry also went left. No point in rocking the boat.

'This is like a roller-coaster, whoa, my legs,' she cried, racing down a dip and back up the other side.

Harry chose not to race. It felt nothing like a roller-coaster.

And still they walked. And walked. And walked. And still Deepika talked. And talked. And talked. And Mum kept stopping to take photos. And they all had to wait each time while she lined up the perfect shot.

'Ow!' Harry slapped at a fly the size of a jumbo jet. He tried to look mournful. It wasn't hard.

'Mum,' Deepika asked. 'Can me and Harry go ahead, just for a bit?'

Harry wasn't sure he wanted to go ahead. But he didn't want to wait here either. Mum was taking selfies with what Ana claimed was an orchid. It looked more like a dried spider on a stick.

'What do you think, Charl?' Ana asked. 'Can the kids go a little way ahead?'

Mum hardly looked up. 'Sure, okay.' She lined up another photo.

'Yay!' Deepika cheered.

'Just five minutes,' Ana warned. 'Then you stop and wait for us.'

'Okay,' chimed Deepika, and she winked at Harry.

Harry was too surprised to wink back.

While Mum posed for another awkward orchid selfie, Harry and Deepika set out. Now he didn't have to concentrate on looking miserable for Mum, he felt a bit lighter. Then he remembered the three-walled hut. Mum had tried to hide her shock when Ana had revealed that little detail in the car. 'Just three walls?' Mum'd asked, turning pale.

Ana had grinned. 'You only need three — the important bit's the roof.'

Harry walked behind Deepika, trying to imagine sleeping in a hut with only three walls. He wasn't even sure it could work.

When Deepika stopped, he nearly walked into the back of her. She turned to check that their mothers were out of sight, then she grinned. 'You want a chocolate frog?'

Harry nodded carefully. 'Okay.'

'Top pocket,' she said, turning so he could reach the zipper on her bag. 'Quick. Mum'll say it's too soon for a snack. But it's never too soon for chocolate.'

He set to work, finding the packet and dishing out a frog each. Deepika eyed him curiously as she bit off her frog's head. 'You're really quiet.'

Harry bit off his own frog's head, chewing hard.

'You want a turn in the lead?' she asked him.

He shrugged. The lead. Whatever.

'You'll love it,' said Deepika. 'I do.' And she grinned right at him.

Maybe it was the frog, but her smile made Harry feel stronger and braver and chocolatey. How hard could it be, being in the lead?

'All right,' he said, and Deepika cheered.

All he had to do was follow the track. It twisted and turned ahead of him, a pale ribbon of sand on a desiccated ocean. And so whatever. He could walk along a track.

Harry adjusted his bag and started out, in the lead. He'd show Deepika just how easy it could be.

UNDER ATTACK

Harry walked fast and they pulled ahead of
the mums. He was puffing, and his left toe was
rubbing, but they were really racing and he was
almost starting to enjoy this whole hiking thing.
That's when he saw the snake.

It wasn't on a yellow triangle, tacked onto the
bark of a tree. It was lying half on the track, half in
the bushes, soaking up the sun.

It took him less than a second to start
screaming. He backed away, smashing into
Deepika and knocking them both to the ground.
'Snake! Snake!'

Deepika twisted for a better look, wrestling with his body and their packs to get a glimpse of the threat.

It was still there, its scaly body half-on and half-off the track. How fast could a snake move? Did snakes chase you? Sometimes ants could chase you. Probably snakes could too. 'Snake,' he repeated, breathless and squeaky and pointing right at it.

'Shhh …' Deepika's voice was quiet and tense. She held an urgent finger to her lips. 'We need to get up. Slowly.'

Silently, carefully, they untangled and scrambled to their feet. Harry didn't take his eyes off the snake. Why hadn't it moved? Perhaps it was dead. Or maybe it was gathering its strength.

'Now we back away,' Deepika whispered, her fingers guiding him into reverse.

The only sound was Harry's panicked breath.

Then he tripped over a root, screamed, and fell

writhing to the ground.

Deepika grabbed his arm and tried to haul him up. 'It's on the move!' she gasped. 'Quick!' And then she collapsed to the ground, too, wheezing. It was an incredulous, delirious sort of sound.

Was she bitten?

But no, she was laughing, and looking relieved. 'Not a snake,' she said. 'A goanna. Look.'

There, further down the track but now right in the middle, was a lizard. Its long, striped tail looked exactly like a snake.

'Goannas are fine,' said Deepika. 'They're not poisonous.'

'Do they attack?' Harry croaked.

'Not unless they think you're a tree.' Deepika grinned. 'I was so scared, Harry. I was so, so scared.'

He'd been pretty scared too, but he'd never admit it. Then he remembered how he'd screamed and fallen to the ground, and he figured Deepika already knew. 'Me too,' he said.

By a lizard.

Harry looked at Deepika and she looked at him and they both just started laughing. Their laughter spooked the goanna and it raced off into the bushes, its snake-like tail following quickly after. It ran like a hula-hooping knock-kneed miniature crocodile, which made Harry laugh even more.

Just then Ana arrived, making them jump. Harry braced himself, ready for Deepika to tell the oh-so-hilarious story of how Harry had screamed and collapsed and mistaken a lizard's tail for a snake.

But all she said was 'Hey, Mum.'

'Hey, you two.' Ana looked at them both, seeming to sense something was up. 'All okay here? I thought I heard something.'

'All good,' grinned Deepika.

Harry flashed her a grateful smile.

Then Mum arrived, panting. 'Harry!' she called.

'I have to show you these photos.' She waved her phone at him, flicking through shots. 'Look at this amazing tree. And that sky. And this rock.'

Harry wanted to point out that they were surrounded by amazing trees and sky and rocks. He also wanted to explain that if he'd had his phone, he could've taken an amazing photo of the goanna. But that required telling the story. And after facing off with a man-eating lizard-snake, all this talking about photos was pretty boring. So was having to sulk about his phone.

Soon they were walking again, but Harry and Deepika didn't get too far ahead before Harry heard something beep from behind him. His heart fell.

Mum whooped with surprise. 'Oh! Reception! Harry, wait a second darling, come back a wee way. Looks like we've got some reception.'

Mum's phone beeped again and again as her messages came through, one after the other. She stopped right where she was, under the baking sun, totally engrossed.

Harry and Deepika backtracked a short way to the shade of a tree. Ana joined them, and after a minute, she heaved off her pack. 'Come into the shade, Charl,' she called to Mum.

Mum looked up. 'I will, I just have to …' She looked down again.

Unbelievable. So, Harry couldn't bring his phone, but she could use hers whenever she liked? Harry tried to catch Mum's eye, so she'd realise the situation. But she only had eyes for her phone.

Ana shifted uncomfortably. 'Okay. Well …' She looked at Harry and Deepika. 'It's a bit soon for a snack. I don't suppose you guys are hungry?'

Harry and Deepika exchanged a look and Harry tried not to laugh. 'Starving,' he said, and slumped in the tree's delicious shade. Deepika dropped down next to him, digging in her pack for the jelly snakes. She offered him first pick, so he grabbed a red one. Usually he bit off their heads, but this time he started with the tail.

Ten minutes later they were still waiting. Even a second snake didn't help. And the third just made Harry feel sick.

'Oh,' Mum frowned at her phone, stabbing with her fingers. She'd joined them in the tree's shade, but this only seemed to have increased her email endurance. Now she huffed. 'Can't they do anything right?' She looked up, face apologetic. 'Sorry, I just have to …'

Five minutes after that, Deepika sighed, stretching a yellow snake from her teeth like a piece of elastic straw. 'Can we go ahead, Mum? I mean properly ahead. Not just five minutes. Pleeeease?'

Ana took a swig of water, watching Mum on her phone. So far she'd been pretty strict about everyone staying within minutes of each other. 'At the pace of the slowest hiker,' she'd insisted. But since that hiker was addicted to selfies and email, the pace was painfully slow. They were constantly waiting for Mum to catch up.

'We'll be totally responsible,' said Deepika. 'And we'll be safe, because we can use the walkie-talkies, can't we Harry?'

What? This was the first Harry had heard of walkie-talkies.

'Remember?' said Deepika. 'I was telling you, on the way up.'

Ah. Walkie-talkies. Right. Harry just nodded and tried to look like a good listener.

'Pleeeeease,' said Deepika. She turned the full force of her enormous smile onto her mum.

Ana looked resigned and pulled out a map, studying the twist of wriggling lines. 'This could be a great lunch spot,' she said, pointing. 'There could even be views.' She looked at Harry and Deepika, as if assessing them. 'You can go ahead and find somewhere to stop for lunch, and we'll meet you there. What do you think?'

The only maps Harry could read were in computer games, but Deepika nodded enthusiastically.

Ana looked across to where Mum was still gawping at her phone. 'Charl?' she asked.

Mum looked up. 'Sorry, this won't take ...'

'Do you mind if the kids go ahead? Just to the top of the hill?'

Mum actually looked at them then. Harry was too excited about going ahead to bother looking sad about his phone. He readjusted his pack and tried to look fresh and ready, as if all his life he'd dreamed of a hiking holiday.

Mum did a half-nod-half-shrug at Ana, and Ana pulled two walkie-talkies from her pack. 'One for you,' she said to Deepika. 'And one for us. Treat them carefully, they're not toys.'

Deepika held a handset to her mouth. 'Testing, testing,' she said. 'This is not a drill. Over.'

· Her voice broadcast through Ana's handset. 'I

read you,' said Ana. 'And this *is* a drill. So …' She turned to Mum. 'What do you think? The kids can use theirs to stay in touch. They're good for up to a kilometre away.'

Mum flicked her eyes to Harry's, then back to her phone, then back to Harry. He tried to imagine the war raging in her head. She'd be torn between concern for her only child, and concern that she'd miss someone's message. He already knew which would win.

'Sounds great,' she said. 'Just not too far, okay?'

'Okay,' said Harry, smiling his thanks. Though what was the point? He was already looking at the top of Mum's head.

Ana spoke into her walkie-talkie. 'Watch for Waugal markers,' she said.

'Roger that,' Deepika radioed back. 'Over.'

'And stick together,' radioed Ana. Then she spoke without the walkie-talkie, which made it seem more serious. 'And no running. All this pea gravel makes it easy to fall. Take it easy, okay?'

Deepika nodded furiously. Harry tried to appear competent.

'See you at lunch,' said Deepika. 'Over.'

'See you at lunch,' agreed Ana. 'Over and out.'

'Bye Mum,' said Harry.

'Bye,' mumbled Mum. 'I'll just be a minute …'

So Deepika and Harry set off, for real this time, just the two of them, entirely alone, and even after the first step it felt different.

Of course, they weren't really alone. Mum and Ana were right behind, just as they'd always been, because there was only one track and they were all on it. But somehow now it felt like an entirely different adventure. As if Deepika and Harry were the only two people on the whole planet. And all the trees and all the rocks and all the animals were a special part of their private and wild and incredible world.

'Yes!' crowed Deepika, the moment they were

out of earshot.

Harry just breathed it all in. They walked and Deepika talked and Harry hardly noticed his backpack, or the heat. And sometimes, when Deepika literally jumped over fallen branches, Harry jumped too.

SNOTTYGOBBLE

They'd been walking only a few minutes when
Deepika spotted the next black-and-yellow triangle
on a nearby tree. 'Waugal,' she said. She pressed the
walkie-talkie button. 'We're on track, over.'

Ana's voice chimed through, steady and
confident. 'Great stuff. Over.'

They slogged up the hill, Harry's heart pumping
hard and his left heel rubbing like crazy. He
wondered briefly whether his feet might wear
away, but forgot to care too much. Around them
leaves rustled and birds sang and he felt alive.
Like a mountaineer, breaking new ground in an
unexplored land.

He didn't even mind that Deepika talked so much. In fact, it was sometimes kind of interesting. She seemed to know all the names of all the flowers and all the rocks and probably all the ants too. Every single one. *That's Michael*, he imagined her saying. *And that's Matilda.*

'That's a wandoo,' she said, pointing at a tree. 'See its bark flaking off? And that's from an emu,' she said, pointing at a chunky dollop of super-gross poo. 'See how it's full of seeds? And they're carnivorous flowers.' She showed Harry some tiny pincushions that shone with beads of sticky dew. 'But don't worry,' she grinned, 'they only eat insects.'

Soon they were hiking up and alongside another sunny ridge. The day's heat rose in waves around them, the song of crickets rang out. Even the feel of the path had changed. It was less like a sandpit and more a mosaic of coloured leaves and rusty soil. And there were flowers everywhere, white and yellow, purple and red, and even blue.

Deepika pointed at a tree oozing sap into a puddle on the ground. 'That's a marri,' she said. 'They make the honky nuts, plus you can use their flowers to make tea. And did you know that marri means blood?'

Harry gulped. It did look like blood, slowly dripping down to the forest floor. For some reason it reminded him of the stolen car and the diamonds.

And then, after maybe half an hour, they reached the top: a huge carpet of granite, rolling across the crest of the hill and edging down the other side. There was a cool breeze and shady trees. There were even rock pools where the last of the rain had collected, and tiny bell-like flowers tufting at the sides. Harry spotted another lizard, smaller this time. Then another. They weren't goannas, they were smaller, the size of bananas, and they watched the walkers from the rocks.

'They're crevice dragons,' said Deepika. 'Check

it out.' She turned to one and spoke right to it. 'Is this the top, dragon?' The lizard bobbed its head up and down. Harry couldn't believe it.

'You think we're total legends, dragon?' she asked, and it bobbed up and down again. Harry laughed.

'You think it's time for more chocolate?' she asked the lizard, but it scampered away, disappearing into the twists and folds of the rock. 'Well, *I* think it's time for chocolate,' she said, and Harry agreed.

'I'll grab the frogs, you tell the parents we're here,' said Deepika, offering him the walkie-talkie.

They plonked themselves onto the sun-warmed rock. He could see all the way across the world, right into the green of the valley. They'd done it! They'd climbed the mountain. Alone. And he still had most of his feet. Nothing had ever felt better.

He radioed the good news. 'Made it. Waiting for lunch delivery, over.'

'Roger that,' came the reply. 'Well done.'

Harry beamed. Deepika handed him another frog. 'Now, try this,' she said, jumping to her feet. She began walking across the rock with a bounce in her feet, like an astronaut on the moon. 'Feels like you're floating. It's because you're used to having such a heavy pack, and then suddenly you don't, so it feels really weird …'

She looked really weird, walking like a cartoon character across the rock. But she did seem to be having fun, and there was no one else around …

Harry gave it a try. She was right. It felt like he was floating.

And they were still floating when Mum and Ana arrived.

Ana swung off her pack and pulled out a little cooker. In no time she had a pot of water bubbling away, and soon all four of them were sitting on the breezy rock, spooning curly chicken noodles into their mouths and feasting on the view. Best lunch

ever. Best lunch spot too.

Harry gave Mum a big smile, and she smiled back. And then her phone beeped.

'Oh, that's lucky!' she said. 'I didn't realise we'd have reception here. I just have to …' And that was that.

Phone stuff. Always with the phone stuff. It felt dumb, sitting in the best lunch spot ever, waiting round while Mum checked her phone. It spoiled it somehow. And when Mum looked up, everyone was watching her, even Ana. Mum put her phone away.

'It's only work,' she said. 'I'll get back to them later.'

Harry was impressed.

The rest of lunch was fun. They chatted and ate juicy apples and laughed at the lizards, and when Harry and Deepika asked if they could go ahead again, Mum and Ana actually talked about it and agreed. 'Not too far ahead,' Ana added. 'Stay in range of the walkie-talkies.'

Harry felt as if he could fly all the way to the three-walled hut. He and Deepika took turns in the lead, following the rolling path down into a valley. The ground was covered in ankle-wrecking honky nuts and marble-like pea gravel, but they took their time and stuck together, soon falling into the routine of hiking. Deepika even left some space for Harry to talk, now that he felt like talking. They told jokes and crunched on smarties. They spotted more carnivorous pincushions, plus a plant with tiny white flowers that showered like snowflakes if you bumped into it. And Waugals. Lots of Waugals.

'There's one,' said Harry, pointing to the yellow triangle on a patchworked trunk.

They crossed a dry creek, then found an ancient tree so enormous they couldn't reach around it, not even when they joined hands to try. And a clearing with moss so soft Harry wanted to try it out for a pillow. Then they came to the sickly smell of something dead.

'Maybe a roo,' said Deepika. 'Come on, let's get past.'

They covered their noses and ran along the track, trying not to breathe. Harry imagined the roo, rotten and bloated and crawling with flies. That sort of thing could happen, out here in the bush.

But soon the stench was gone and the air everywhere was sweet.

The walkie-talkie crackled. 'You guys okay?' came Ana's voice.

'Yep,' Deepika answered. 'All good, over.'

'Great stuff,' answered Ana.

And on they walked.

'Waugal,' said Deepika, pointing to another marker. Then she pointed to a vivid-green tree with a shady umbrella. 'And that's a snottygobble,' she announced.

'It's so not,' said Harry.

'It so is,' she grinned. 'It even has snotty fruit, like jelly beans, look. You can eat them … wanna try?'

'After you,' said Harry, but neither of them did.

They spent a while exploring the hollowed remains of a burned-out forest giant. Inside the trunk was space enough to fit them both, and several spiders too, so they didn't stay long. 'It's still growing,' marvelled Harry, staring up. And it was, still green and tall and reaching for the clouds.

They walked on and on, spotting Waugals as they went. 'Check this out,' Deepika said, stopping beside a sapling gum. 'You can make a whistle from the leaves, the red ones, you just fold them back, like this …'

She showed him how to crease a newborn leaf to reveal its stretchy membrane, then they made the worst shrieking sounds ever by curling a leaf into their tongues. Harry was glad Mum wasn't around to tell them to stop that dreadful racket.

Soon the track left the bush and joined a wider, unsealed road.

'An old firebreak,' guessed Deepika.

'Any Waugal?' Harry asked.

Deepika pointed at the black-and-yellow snake that led their way. Beyond the marker, the dirt road rose steeply uphill. 'Let's make an arrow,' she said, 'so they know we've gone the right way.'

They spent a few minutes gathering some honky-nut-sized rocks and arranging them into a neat little arrow that pointed the same way as the Waugal. Then they made an H and D to go with it. 'So they know it's us,' said Deepika, dusting the orange dirt from her hands and onto her trousers.

'We left you an arrow, over,' radioed Harry, as they walked away.

There was a pause, rather a long pause.

At last Ana's strained, static voice came through. 'We'll be with you in a bit. There's just some urgent email, over.' He could almost hear the eye-roll in her voice.

'Roger,' said Harry. 'Over and out.' He turned to Deepika and made a brave sort of face. She made a wacky face back, and it made him smile. It was nice that she understood. He felt like maybe they'd been friends for ages, not just a morning's walk.

'Do you remember,' he said suddenly. 'Right at the start. The red car, I mean.'

Deepika lowered her voice. 'The first time I ever went hiking, I saw a car like that, just parked in the bush, and I thought maybe it might be stolen,' she confided.

'I know, right,' Harry whispered. 'Why else would you hide an entire car?'

'I know, right,' whispered Deepika. 'Where do you think he is now, the driver, I mean?'

They stopped to look around. It was so quiet, and the heaviness of empty bush seemed to press around them. The miles and miles of trees and scrub and dirt began to shimmer and loom and

Harry's heart beat faster. But it was dumb to worry. It was also dumb that they were whispering. The driver was probably just a hiker, Ana said so, and she knew everything about everything about hiking.

'Race you to the top,' he said. Because there was no way you could worry about red cars or mysterious drivers when you were scrambling up a hill. And there was no way you could fall either. Whoever heard of falling up? It was the perfect distraction.

They laughed and raced and puffed, and it was like running on ice, thrillingly steep and incredibly slippery. They stayed neck and neck, arriving at the top triumphant, with hands and shins scratched and faces glowing.

'Great view!' said Deepika. 'Snake?' They were all out of frogs.

They shared the last of the jelly snakes as they walked. They chewed and made up jokes and the hill didn't seem so steep, not now they were at the top. Soon they were faced with coming down the other side, and it seemed even worse. In places the hard dirt was layered with pea gravel, in others rain had eroded the ground into jagged channels, eating it away like termites into wood. They scooted down on their bums, chatting and chewing and using their hands as anchors, sometimes pausing to roll rocks down the crooked gutters, making bets on how far each rock would go.

'If it started raining right now,' said Harry, 'this whole hill would turn to mud, and we'd probably sink into quicksand and never be seen again.'

Deepika grinned. 'If it started raining right now, we could make a raft from all the trees and sail it down the hill like a mudslide, all the way to the ocean.'

Harry looked around. 'Which way is the ocean, anyway?'

Deepika shrugged. They were a long way from

any ocean. 'You hungry for chips?'

At the bottom of the hill they threw off their packs and dug around for the chips. Then they sat right in the middle of the dirt road to eat them. Because there was no way cars could really use it as a road. It was too steep and washed away. And they didn't want to waste time looking for a prettier spot. They were hungry now.

The chips were just original, not Harry's all-time fave, salt-and-vinegar, but for some reason they tasted incredible. Crunchy and super-salty. Harry spaced them out with swigs of water, secretly glad Ana had made him carry so much.

Deepika pressed the walkie-talkie button. 'Did you see our arrow yet? Over.'

They grabbed a handful of chips, munching while they waited for a reply. None came. The wind washed like water through the treetops. Deepika asked again, but there was no answer.

'They must be out of range,' she said.

Harry just shrugged and poked at his shoes. It hurt that his mum couldn't spend five minutes without checking her phone. It hurt worse than his blistering heel. 'They won't be long, they're probably just over the hill.'

They ate a few more chips, then Deepika tried again. 'Why did the emu cross the road? Over.'

There was no answer.

'Why?' Harry asked.

'To prove he wasn't a chicken,' she said.

Harry groaned and rolled around on the ground.

Deepika's brown eyes danced as she watched Harry over the top of the handset. She pressed the button. 'What kind of music do kangaroos listen to? Over.'

But he knew this one. 'Hip hop,' he said.

She laughed and his heart leapt. 'Nice,' she said. 'And hopera. Get it? Over.' She lowered the walkie-talkie. 'Hop-era.'

They both laughed now, the sound swallowed into the nothingness of bush.

There was still no response on the walkie-talkie. Harry felt a kind of worry grip his stomach. Probably too many chips.

Deepika tried again. 'Why did the emu cross the road? Over.'

They waited a while longer, then Harry stood and stretched, looking up and down the road. Into the surrounding bush. No sign of Mum or Ana. No sign of anyone.

And no sign of a sign, either. Not even a Waugal. He gulped. Icy cold shot up and down his limbs, despite the sun. Surely his mum couldn't spend *this* long checking messages. Surely she cared at least a bit about where they'd got to. About non-phone stuff. About making it to the hut in time for marshmallows and more noodles and all the fun stuff Deepika had been telling him about.

He looked around, wondering how much

farther the hut would be. Wondering how far they'd already come.

There should at least be a trail marker.

When was the last time he'd seen a Waugal, anyway?

WAITING FOR A SIGN

Ages. That's how long since he'd last seen a Waugal. Ages. Maybe way back at the top of the hill? Or maybe before that, back at the dry creek? Or by the giant tree? Or …

Or maybe they were lost.

Harry instructed himself to relax. No point freaking out. Deepika had probably been keeping track of Waugals. She did this sort of thing all the time, hiking, and adventure stuff. She knew to watch for trail markers.

So they were almost certainly not lost. All the same …

'We should probably go back,' he said. 'Just till

the walkie-talkies are in range.' He'd feel better when they could hear Ana's or Mum's voice.

Deepika offered him the handset. 'You wanna try?'

Harry tried not to seem desperate. 'Hello? Mum? Do you read me? Ana?'

Silence trickled into the space between them. Then it filled up that space and began to spread, stretching into the trees and then the sky, devouring everything, till Harry wondered what might be eaten up next.

Then, finally, he spoke. 'They're probably really close by now. She can't have that many messages.' It was sort of a joke, but not a very good one.

Then they just sat, side by side, waiting for their parents to catch up. *Not too far ahead.* That's what Ana had said.

Half an hour, Harry promised himself. That's how long they'd wait. He didn't have his phone though, so he wouldn't know when half an hour was up. *Stay calm*, he told himself. *Stay calm.*

They waited forever, seriously, actually, forever. They listened to the wind in the leaves, birds singing from the trees. They watched giant ants scurry for chip crumbs. They rolled pea gravel along the track. But that was all there was. No cars, no footsteps. No non-stop chatter or requests to pose with this flower or that leaf. They just sat and sat and sat, till Harry began to feel cold.

Then Deepika cleared her throat in an odd kind of way. 'So,' she said. 'When was the last time you saw a Waugal?'

Harry kept his eyes on the ants. Crickets chirped but the silence stretched.

Deepika threw a fistful of gravel at the track. It scattered and bounced then fell still, mingling with the dirt road, so you couldn't see which bits were new, and which had been there all along. 'Me too,' she said.

They looked at each other. It was awful, the

quiet and the waiting and the cold that was settling in Harry's heart. 'Maybe we should go back.'

Without a word, they hoisted the heavy bags onto their backs and began the long climb back to the top of the hill, retracing their footsteps up and along the gravel road. They climbed past all the ruts and dry rivulets and pea gravel traps. No Waugal.

They scrambled back down the other side of the super-steep hill, the one they'd raced up. It was almost impossible to walk down, so they didn't bother. Instead they half-ran, half-rolled. Their shoes slid like skates and the pea gravel was like polished ice. The honky nuts were like wheels and soon they were going too fast. Deepika slipped twice and grazed her hands, but she didn't say a thing. Neither did Harry when he slipped and grazed his elbows. And still there was no Waugal. No Mum. No Ana.

Why weren't they coming along the trail? Harry

remembered the smell of something dead along the track. He began to feel ill.

Then they found their arrow, the one they'd made by arranging rocks, and they found their H and D as well. All their rocks were still there, untouched, still marking the point where the track left the bush and joined the old gravel road. The Waugal they'd spotted was there too, pointing in the direction they'd just come from. So they weren't lost.

But where were the mums?

Harry started a slow panic.

'Maybe they made a mistake, went the wrong way?' he suggested. Except they wouldn't. There was the arrow, and the Waugal. And Ana knew about these things. 'Or maybe …'

He spun, searching for answers, as if their mums might be hiding in the trees. And then he saw it.

A Waugal. Another Waugal. The Waugal they'd

missed. Deepika saw it too.

It was only a few metres along the gravel road, but on the other side, tacked to a tree about five metres into the bush, on the left. The Waugal was the right colour. It was the right size. And it marked the thin, winding trail as it turned off the dirt road and dived back into the thick of the bush.

They'd missed it. They'd been so busy climbing the hill, so busy beheading snakes and telling jokes, they'd totally missed the track.

Harry thought about being alone in the middle of such an enormous chunk of uncharted wilderness, and refused to cry. Deepika sucked on her bottom lip. There was just one thing for it.

'We better be quick,' she said.

He nodded. It was the only way. Thank goodness they still had their packs.

They took turns in the lead. They walked faster, heaps faster than Mum and Ana could ever manage. They had a good chance of catching up before their parents even realised they'd been lost.

They raced off the dirt road and into the thick bush, following the Waugal, always following the Waugal. Harry's muscles pumped harder, his shoe rubbed faster. But they had to go fast, because they'd been sitting for ages, just waiting for their mums to catch up. And all along it'd been Harry and Deepika who'd been left behind.

Soon he was breathing hard and feeling better. Something about putting one foot in front of the other seemed to lift his sad, sick mood. There was something about the bush, alive and rustling around him, and the comfort of the path, as it moved and changed beneath his feet. And there were Waugals on loads of trees. They were on the right track. It was going to be okay.

'They're going to freak when we find them,' Deepika puffed from behind him. 'We could be like, "Boo!" and they'd be all amazed.'

Harry grinned, but didn't stop walking.

'We could pretend to be tigers,' said Deepika. 'Or gorillas.'

'Or wild pigs,' said Harry.

Except wild pigs weren't so funny.

Something grabbed him across the face. He yelled, throwing his hands up to protect himself. Nothing.

'You okay?' Deepika asked.

'Spider web,' he said, pulling the sticky web from his face. 'Gross.'

'Yeah, gross,' she said, looking nervous. 'Come on. Before it starts getting dark.'

After that they walked in silence, except for when they spotted a Waugal.

Harry imagined his left heel and little toe might wear completely away. He wondered whether the pain might stop if they did wear away. But it only got worse.

The afternoon seemed horribly hot. Flies buzzed at Harry's face. And his shoulders hurt

from carrying his pack. Which, incidentally, was way heavier than he'd thought at the start.

What was in there, anyway? Harry's sleeping bag wouldn't fit, not even after Ana had repacked it into a tiny stuff sack. She'd had to shove it into her own pack and she'd given him another super-daggy spare jumper to carry instead. So now all he had was … He tried to work it out. His water bottle. Two spare jumpers. Muesli bars. Too many warm socks. Some seaweed crackers … That was it.

Perhaps Ana snuck in something extra? Like slippers made of lead? He wouldn't put it past her.

He was deep in thought when Deepika cried out.

'We're here!'

She turned to him, brown face flushed and happy. Ahead of her, on the edge of the track, was a low, wooden sign showing a silhouette of a man and a woman. A toilet.

Harry was happy to find a toilet. He'd been

busting for ages, only he didn't like to mention it. But all the same, he'd been hoping for a hut, even one with only three walls.

Then Deepika pointed beyond the toilet sign, into the distance. There, fading into the shimmer of the trees, was the unmistakable line of a roof. A dark green, corrugated roof. The hut! The actual hut! They really had made it.

Deepika and Harry ran the last stretch, calling out as they went.

'Mum!'

'Mum! We're here!'

Harry hoped they weren't frantic. 'Mu-um! We made it!'

There was no answer.

And when they burst from the track, into full sight of the hut, there was no sign that anyone had ever been there. No heavy packs discarded out the front. No tired hikers relaxing in the last of the sun. No cooker or hot, curly noodles. Just a couple of wooden picnic tables. A concrete fire pit. And the hut, made of wood, complete with the promised three sides.

Harry could see right inside.

It was empty.

AT THE HUT

Harry took off his bag and placed it on the picnic table.

'They must be hiding,' Deepika decided. She dumped her pack on the gravelly ground and began searching around the hut.

But there weren't many places to hide, and Harry couldn't remember the last time Mum had played hide-and-seek. He gulped. The hut was as big as his bedroom, which wasn't saying much. It had bare plywood floors, and on either side were raised plywood platforms, also empty.

And that was it. No mattresses. No kitchen. No mums.

Harry guessed the raised platforms were some sort of bunk, for people who liked heights and despised comfort. Ana had mentioned three walls, but not barbaric beds. And she'd also mentioned she was going to be there too, with Harry's mum, at the hut, all of them together.

Deepika returned from her search. 'They're not here.'

Harry nodded. Suddenly it seemed incredibly dumb to have raced so fast to get here.

He felt for the walkie-talkie in his pocket.

'Want to call again?' Deepika asked.

In a flash he was pressing its button. 'Hello? Are you there?'

Nothing.

'You forgot to say "over",' said Deepika.

'Over,' said Harry.

But it made no difference.

They sat for a while, listening to the dusk creeping closer. The sounds of the bush were changing, the shadows growing longer. Harry wondered what happened to the hut on the days when no one was there. What did it do, when there was no one in it to cook noodles and toast marshmallows? And what about all the animals and birds? What did they do? All the creatures with private, busy lives, all the trees with no one to ever pass them by. What if Harry and Deepika were the only two people left in the world?

Harry was used to being alone. He spent hours alone every day, in his room, playing games and watching TV. But this was a different type of alone. Even with Deepika there beside him, he felt abandoned. This kind of alone was somehow perilous, as if the sheer scale of the bush was enough to swallow them up. Would they ever be heard from again?

'Maybe we should get things ready,' Deepika said. 'For when our mums get here.'

She was right. Of course, she was right. Mum

and Ana would be here soon, and doing a few jobs now would make it easier for when they arrived tired and hungry. They could get started now, prepare the camp. Mum might even be impressed with all the jobs they'd done. But there was one thing Harry had to deal with first. It was becoming increasingly urgent. There could be no further delay.

'I gotta go pee.'

Deepika nodded. 'Me too.'

They set off, backtracking fifty or so metres to the sign with the silhouettes. Harry wondered how many toilets there would be.

It turned out there was only one. It did have four walls, but that was the most you could say.

'It's a pit dunny,' explained Deepika. 'A long drop. No flush. No water either. Hopefully some loo paper.' She raised an eyebrow at Harry, as if daring him to freak out.

He tried to stay calm. It was dark, sure. And

small. Yep. And … But that couldn't be right. It locked on the outside. What kind of toilet locked on the outside? 'You go first,' he said.

A few minutes later, they were both done. Harry had held his breath for as long as possible, but it hadn't been all that bad. 'Like a waterfall,' Harry grinned.

'You're gross,' said Deepika, making a face, and he laughed.

After that they set to work. Deepika arranged her sleeping bag and snacks. Harry unpacked the super-daggy spare jumpers, plus his own warm clothes and socks. They saved the seaweed crackers but ate the rest of the chips. Then they washed it all down with almost the last of their water.

'Not all of it,' Deepika said. 'Just in case.'

Harry nodded. Ana had warned them earlier. 'Don't drink any creek water, and we'll need to treat the tank water too.' Then she'd listed a bunch of exotic microbes that could rake your intestines clean, or turn your number twos into recurring fractions. It hadn't sounded fun.

In good news, he'd discovered a whole extra bottle of drinking water in his pack. *Thanks Ana!* The water was heavy, but loads better than concrete slippers. He and Deepika put it carefully with what remained of their snacks. Then they unpacked a clear plastic tub they'd discovered in a corner of the hut.

'It's the hut logbook,' said Deepika, flicking through the pages of a battered green book. 'Every hut has them. You write where you're from, and where you're going, stuff like that.'

Deepika checked the rest of the box while Harry carefully scribed their names into the log:

Name: Harry and Deepika, Charlene and Ana
From: Car park
To: Hut
Nights: 1

'What shall I put for the comments?' he asked.

Deepika had piled up half a dozen tealight candles, an ancient packet of matches, a couple of ballpoint pens, and some track brochures … 'Let's wait,' she said. 'Till they get here.'

For a while they pored over the logbook entries, reading out the details and secrets of other people's adventures. Some had hiked through rainstorms and mud. Others had sunburned to a crisp. Many had hiked with friends. Others had journeyed completely alone. Harry couldn't imagine it.

'Here's one,' said Deepika. ' "Loved the peace and quiet," ' she read, ' "and the nocturnal visitor". She frowned and looked across. 'What do you reckon that means?'

Harry shrugged. Probably a park ranger. Probably not a kidnapper. 'Maybe a Mr Whippy van,' he joked. But that reminded him of the red car.

'Well, hopefully it was a friendly visitor,' said Deepika, pretending she was joking too.

'Weird,' said Harry suddenly. Because thinking of the red car had made him realise … According to the logbook, no one had visited their hut in three days, not even a Mr Whippy van. And that seemed a long time, especially if the red car was supposed to belong to a hiker.

'Maybe red-car-guy is hiking the other way,' Harry suggested. That was probably it. The track ran north–south, and they were hiking north. So red-car-guy would be hiking south. That could happen.

Deepika stood up. 'Let's go find firewood. Mum's bringing marshmallows. We could prepare the wood, so it'll all be ready.'

Great idea. Soon they had a pile of deadwood as big as themselves, stacked up next to the concrete fire pit. It was a great way to stay busy, plus daylight was fading and it would be tricky to find wood if the mums were much longer.

The sounds of the bush continued to change. The temperature dropped. The sun fell dangerously close to the trees.

And where were their parents anyway? They should be here. They should all be eating noodles and preparing marshmallow sticks.

Harry sighed. They'd unpacked their stuff, read the logbook, gathered wood for the fire. Mum should be here by now.

He reached for the walkie-talkie. It was only about the fiftieth time. 'Hello? Are you there? Over.'

It was always the same question. And always the same response. Silence.

He put on his warm jumper. Deepika put on hers too. And suddenly it was dark, properly dark. Deepika had a torch, but that didn't seem enough. They talked about lighting the fire, but that seemed too much. Even in a concrete fire pit, starting a fire just didn't seem right. Not when they were so alone.

In the end, they used the ancient matches from the hut box to light a couple of mini candles, one each. The flames flickered, casting a cheery light across the table, though Harry felt anything but cheery. They tried telling jokes, but nothing was funny.

'Should we go back?' Harry asked.

Deepika's eyes glowed in the candlelight. 'It's pretty dark,' she said hesitantly.

Agreed. They should stay in the same place. That's what you were supposed to do when you were lost. Deepika knew this stuff. She knew what to do.

Except they weren't lost. They knew exactly where they were. It was Mum and Ana who were lost.

'Should we go find them?' Deepika asked.

Harry looked beyond the candlelight to the haphazard shapes of rustling trees. 'It *is* pretty dark.'

He looked over their belongings. They had Deepika's sleeping bag, the spare jumpers, two rain jackets and three pairs of warm socks. Plus some smarties and a bottle of water.

He was super-grateful for the extra water, seriously. But if he was going to be fussy, it would've been fab to also have his sleeping bag. And another packet of crackers. And some sort of roast dinner. The kind with steaming potatoes and really amazing gravy, and crunchy green peas. He would even eat peas.

'Smartie?' offered Deepika.

They spread out what was left of the smartie packet on the lid of the plastic tub, then divided them equally. There was an extra blue one left over. They decided to save it.

A VISITOR

'Hello Mum? Ana? Can anyone hear me?'

Harry tried again, from inside the wrappings of
their cosy nest. The nest had been Deepika's idea. If
you're lost in the bush, it's important to stay warm,
she said. This was apparently part of Ana's regular
lecture. And it was an easy part to remember. It
had been stinking hot in the day, but the night's
chill was setting in.

Their nest wasn't great, but it was the best
they could manage. They'd built it at the back of
the hut, in the corner. They'd unzipped Deepika's
sleeping bag, lined the wooden floor with the spare
jumpers, and propped the whole thing together

with their packs. Plus there'd been the spare socks, so they were wearing socks on their hands and even on their feet. That way, one hand remained free, per person. Perfect for the walkie-talkie.

But there was no answer, again. Deepika sighed. 'Maybe their batteries are dead?'

'Maybe they accidentally turned it off?' Harry said.

Deepika sat up, grabbing for the walkie-talkie. 'Maybe it's the wrong frequency!'

Of course! Walkie-talkies had to be tuned to each other, like you tuned to radio stations. 'I thought we agreed on 7,' said Harry.

'We did,' rushed Deepika. 'Or I'm pretty sure we did. But maybe they changed the channel.' She began clicking through channels. There seemed to be dozens.

Maybe Mum and Ana were calling them right now, but on channel 6 or 8, or 27, or something. It was a comforting thought, and Harry held it tight.

Deepika began clicking through each channel, waiting just a few seconds between clicks. There were eighty channels, could you believe it? Whoever needed eighty channels on a walkie-talkie. It wasn't like it was a TV.

They waited and listened to first one channel, then the next. But each of the eighty was silent.

'Maybe we missed one,' said Harry, so they went through them all again, saying 'Hello?' and 'Can anyone hear me?' and waiting longer between clicks each time.

But still there was nothing. Not even a truckie, or some road workers, or like aliens or anything. They must be too far out of range.

Because they were in the middle of the bush. Entirely, completely, totally alone. And because where was Mum? And because why wasn't she here?

And because what if —

A twig snapped. Harry gulped.

Outside their nest, from beyond the hut, a twig had snapped. From somewhere deep in the blackness of the night. Harry grabbed Deepika's arm and she grabbed him back. They forgot all about the walkie-talkie. The mini candles flickered on the picnic table, their wavering light stretching just beyond the missing fourth wall. Nothing stood between them and the twig-snapper. Harry strained his eyes into the darkness.

Nothing. So maybe it really was nothing. Maybe it was a branch falling from a tree, or a gust of wind through the leaves. That could happen in the bush. Especially when no one was there.

Then another twig snapped, louder and closer. Probably Mum. Or maybe Ana. But why weren't they calling out? Harry refused to even think about the red car.

Deepika's grip on his arm tightened. He saw a dark shape move slowly, just beyond the yellow of the candlelight. Harry's heart froze.

For a long time, nothing happened. The shape didn't move again, and Harry didn't dare breathe. He remembered that he and Deepika were all alone, in a massive unending swathe of wilderness. The emptiness pressed in, the loneliness pressed in. Then the something moved, all at once, stepping right towards them.

Except they weren't really steps. They were more like … hops.

'It's a roo,' Deepika whispered. Harry thought she was trying for another joke, but she was serious. It really was a kangaroo. Small, and sort of scruffy-looking.

'The nocturnal visitor,' he whispered back.

Nothing moved, then the roo bounced closer, joining them in the candlelight. It stared right at them, black eyes shining, black nose twitching. Harry felt time stretching, from all the way in the past to all the way into the future, and still he didn't breathe.

The roo put its nose to the ground, and Harry relaxed, watching it snuffle around. Then it hopped closer and snuffled some more.

'Must be hungry,' Deepika whispered.

The roo froze, staring right at them. It was so close he could probably reach out and touch it. It could hop right into the hut and join them for dinner, if it wanted. If there was any dinner.

As he watched the roo, somewhere deep inside Harry's heart, a warmth formed. It was amazing, sharing space with this wild creature. It made him feel that maybe the bush wasn't a huge emptiness or terrifying loneliness. Maybe it was a place that furry creatures called home. A place where living things stretched and unfurled. Where life could go on. Because Harry was with a friend, he was warm, and he wasn't that hungry. I mean, he wasn't snuffling around in the dirt for fallen crumbs. At least, not yet, he wasn't. And maybe their parents were perfectly safe, just dealing with some work stuff, and Mum would come racing out of the darkness, clutching her phone and making apologies, like always.

'It'll be all right, you know,' he said to Deepika.

'I know,' she said, and she squeezed his arm with her sock.

The roo watched them some more. They watched it back. It chose to ignore the nesting sock creatures and hopped patiently around the picnic table, as if it had all the time in the world. But it didn't jump into the hut, and Harry was happy with that.

When it hopped away, there was nothing left to watch. The two candles struggled against the night, flickering with the breeze, or maybe running out of wax. Maybe just tired. Harry's loneliness returned, suddenly and desperately.

Where was Mum? Why hadn't she come? Could she really care that much about updating her status and replying to messages? Harry thought of all the times she'd come late to collect him, and his guts turned to stabbing ice. Because even when she was late, she always came.

Except now was too late. She wasn't coming and he knew it. Deepika's mum wasn't coming either. It was too dark. They'd waited too long. Something must've happened.

'What do we do?'

They had half a bottle of water left, and no way of filtering the tank water. They had one blue smartie for dinner, no first-aid kit, no spare sleeping bag, and, most importantly, no spare parents. 'I guess we need to go find them, right?'

Deepika nodded, though she didn't exactly jump from their nest and start walking. 'Now?' she asked carefully. 'Or in the morning?'

In the morning, it'd be easy to see all the Waugals. And any arrows or signs. Plus any man-eating goanna-snakes or flesh-goring pigs. It'd be way less scary if they waited till morning.

Harry looked hopefully at Deepika. She looked hopefully back.

Because it wasn't as if they would sleep.

'Now,' Harry decided. Even if he was offered a featherbed and a belly full of roast lamb and peas, he'd never be able to sleep. Not when their mums could be out there, in trouble and needing them. 'We need to go now.'

Deepika nodded. They still looked at each other, as if waiting for something to change, but nothing did. So Deepika held up a socked hand and they high-fived with thin grins. Then they stood, stretching their cramped limbs and glowing with the instant cold.

Deepika stuffed her sleeping bag into its sack. Harry packed the jumpers they weren't wearing and popped the logbook into its plastic crate. But first he grabbed the pen:

Name: Harry and Deepika, ~~Charlene and Ana~~
From: Car park
To: Hut
Nights: ~~1~~ 0.5
Comment: Hope you enjoy the firewood. Back
soon.

He blew out the remaining candle and returned it carefully to the plastic crate. Deepika used her headtorch to search the hut one last time. Nothing.

'Ready?'

'Guess so,' Deepika said. 'But first I need to pee.'

GULLY TRAP

Harry's guts stabbed with fear, but he gritted his teeth and kept moving. If his shoulders were aching, or his heel and toe were sore, he didn't notice. He was filled to bursting with this night.

Owls hooted and night creatures rustled, and he refused to be scared. The night air was cold but not enough to get through the spare jumpers. Mist bounced off his warm muscles. The crunch of every footstep echoed in the rhythm of his breath. It was going to be okay. Their mums were going to be okay.

The bush felt smaller, now they were moving through it. Now they had a purpose, now they new what they had to do. It was as if the night was guiding them onwards.

Something flashed at them from ahead, something yellow and black, like an eye, vivid and leering and staring down at them in the night.

'Waugal,' hissed Deepika, her headtorch shining into the distance. The reflective trail marker shone back.

Good. Still on track.

Because of the headtorch, Deepika was totally hands-free. And because of not having a torch, Harry was totally torch-free. Luckily, they could see well enough with just one. Deepika led the way, shining her light out in front, and Harry stayed close behind. High above them, rivers of cloud moved across to blanket any stars. The moon glowed behind a ring of vapour.

'Means it's going to rain,' said Deepika.

Harry remembered the waterproof jacket Ana had insisted on packing and felt a dizzying rush of

appreciation and fear. 'Better get a move on.'

Hours passed. And hours. There were no more chocolate frogs, no lolly snakes, no super-crunchy original chips. Harry and Deepika hiked mostly in silence. It didn't seem the time for jokes. He tried not to worry about where Mum might be. He tried not to think about the red car and its missing driver. Sometimes, when he was feeling strong and positive, as if everything would be okay, the surrounding trees seemed to cloak them, to keep them safe. Other times the trees would change, and their bone-white limbs, twisted and dead, seemed to reach for them, straining to claw at their arms and grab at their legs. But so long as they kept to the track, so long as they stayed with the Waugal …

'What was that?' Deepika asked.

'What?'

They stood, listening to the night. *The red car, the red car, the red car.* Harry's head wouldn't stop.

'Probably nothing,' Deepika said. 'Maybe an owl.'

Harry nodded. Owls were a thing.

And they kept moving, nerves all ajangle.

The trickiest parts were the downhills. In the dark it was even harder to see which bits dropped away, and which bits were strewn with pea gravel. They were puffing and sweating and had just hiked free from the bottom of a gully, when they heard another sound.

Something sharp and static, a tortured cross between a wail and a moan and a cry. And it didn't come from the bush. It came from the walkie-talkie.

'Hello?' the sound said.

Deepika grabbed for the button. 'Mum, is that you?'

The walkie-talkie was crackly but distinct. 'Deepika?'

'Mum!'

Deepika ran. Harry was running too, but Deepika surged ahead. 'Mum?' She ran wildly into the night. 'Mum, where are you?'

The walkie-talkie crackled and cried. 'Deepika! Deepika, I'm here!'

They kept running and running until finally they raced around a corner and there she was, lit up in Deepika's torchlight, waving a torch of her own. She was sitting on the side of the track, leaning against her pack and wrapped in her sleeping bag, one leg propped awkwardly out in front.

'Mum!'

'Deepika!' Ana held out her arms. 'Careful,' she said. 'My leg.'

Deepika stepped around the awkward leg and sank into her mum's embrace. They held each other so tightly it made Harry's chest hurt. 'Deepika, I thought I'd lost you …' Ana pulled away, looking at Deepika's face, then pulled her close again. 'I thought …'

'It's okay, Mum,' she said. 'We're here, it's going to be all right.'

Ana didn't let Deepika out of her arms. She smiled first at Deepika, then at Harry, then at Deepika, over and over. 'Oh, thank heavens you're okay. We thought … I couldn't … I just …' She fell silent, still holding Deepika's hand.

Harry almost couldn't stand to look. His body began to tremble. Where was *his* mum? Why wasn't she here? Why hadn't she stayed? How could she have left her friend like that? How could she have left him?

'What happened to your leg?' asked Deepika.

Ana smiled a tight smile. 'Just a twist or a sprain or something. I should be fine.'

'Looks like a break to me, Mum,' said Deepika, touching the leg gingerly. Ana gasped.

Harry just closed his eyes, trying to squeeze away the pinpricks that burned at the back of his eyelids. Mum hadn't stayed. She didn't care.

He heard Ana and Deepika talking but didn't register their words. Then, after forever, he heard himself speak. His voice seemed very small, as if it'd come from a faraway place, as if it'd been squashed and squeezed into such a tight lump that it couldn't really budge from his throat.

'Is Mum at work?' he managed.

Ana breathed out then, all in a rush. 'Oh, no, Harry. No, she's not at work. We found that hiker, the one from the red car. He'd been lost a couple of days. He hadn't carried enough water and then tried to take a short cut.' She shook her head. 'He was in a bad way. We tried phoning for help, but couldn't get through, so someone had to take him back to the car park, to get help.' Ana slowed then, speaking almost apologetically. 'We'd been looking for you,' she said. 'For hours. We tried calling out, the walkie-talkie, everything, but we didn't know how far you'd gone, or if you were lost, or hurt, or …' Her voice trailed off and Harry remembered how he and Deepika had feasted on salty chips, waiting for their parents to arrive.

'We went back to where we'd last seen you,' continued Ana, 'and we waited, calling and calling. We were hoping you'd come find us, when you realised ...'

Harry gulped. They *had* realised. They just hadn't—

'That's when we found Alistair,' she said. 'He heard our voices and came staggering through the trees. Gave us quite a fright, but we were more frightened to see the state of him. We gave him some water and he perked up a little, but someone had to take him for proper help.' She looked across at Harry. 'Your mum volunteered. It was my job to find you.'

He looked down, blinking hard. Mum'd probably jumped at the chance to leave early and get back to civilisation.

'So then I tried to find you,' continued Ana. 'I thought maybe you might've gone on, maybe all the way to the hut ...'

'We did,' burst Deepika, unable to stay silent any longer. 'We did go to the hut, but at first we waited, for you to catch up, and then we realised we weren't even on the track, so we thought you'd be further ahead, and by the time we realised you weren't ...'

Harry gulped, remembering the icicles of fear in his guts.

'I'm afraid I made a mistake,' Ana said sadly. 'I ran to find you, once I figured you might be at the hut. Along an uneven track, wearing a heavy pack, alone and in the dark.' She looked up at Deepika and pulled her in. 'Not incredibly clever.'

'It's okay, Mum,' said Deepika, holding her close. 'You're okay now.'

Harry couldn't stand to look. His whole face felt twisted and broken, and he couldn't look away either. 'Why didn't Mum stay?' he croaked. 'Why doesn't she care?'

'Oh Harry,' said Ana. 'Your mum's a hero.'

Harry swallowed, his face like stone. 'Yeah.

Anything for a photo opportunity.'

'It wasn't like that, Harry,' Ana continued. 'She was so worried, she didn't want to go, but she had to. She'll be doing all she can to help Alistair, then to find you, to find us.' Ana reached out to pull Harry in.

STicKiNg TogETHER

They offered Ana the last blue smartie, but it
turned out she had an entire banquet in her pack.
There were crackers and cheese and a whole log of
not-too-spicy salami, plus loads of warm clothes,
drinking water, a spare torch, and every kind of
first aid you could imagine, except the kind that
makes a broken leg okay to walk on. She even had
her own mobile phone.

Harry could not believe it. 'But you said—'

'I said we needed a phone for emergencies,'
she said, sharing out cheese-and-salami cracker
sandwiches. 'But of course, there's no reception.
Still, we need to let your mum know you're okay.'

She glanced at her leg ruefully. 'And that I'm not.'

'We could help you walk,' Deepika suggested, looking hopeful. 'We could go at the pace of the slowest hiker.'

Ana shook her head. 'I've tried,' she said, grimacing as she shifted. 'I've been trying since I fell. There's no way …'

Deepika only nodded, no trace of her usual grin. So that was that. They'd just have to wait it out till morning, till help came. Harry shivered at the thought.

'But you two should go,' Ana said. 'You've done a great job, making it all this way. And Harry, your mum will be desperate to know you're safe.' She squeezed Deepika's shoulder. 'I'm proud of you. I'm proud of you both.'

Deepika shook her head. 'We need to stick together, you said …'

Ana smiled and squeezed her shoulder again. 'You two need to stick together. You'll be okay. I'll be okay too. You know where I am, and I'm not going anywhere. The sun'll be up soon. I might even be able to get a few good photos.'

But Deepika wouldn't smile. 'You don't understand. We got lost, we missed the Waugal, we nearly lost you …'

Ana kissed her. 'But you found me again. And I'll be okay. I love you, and you're doing a terrific job.' She turned to Harry. 'Now, you'll need more food, extra water, first aid, and how are you doing for warm socks?'

While they talked rain jackets and jumpers, Harry tried to patch up his wounds. He put bandaids on his heel and toe, where there were two mega-juicy blisters. There was nothing he could do about Mum.

A couple of minutes later he and Deepika were loaded up.

'You should've been carrying this stuff all along,' Ana said remorsefully. She held the two sides of Harry's bag together as he slid the zip shut. 'I underestimated you. You're doing such a great job.'

Now Harry's pack felt super-heavy, but his heart was almost light, as if Ana had also packed a super-serve of bubbles.

'Okay then,' she said. 'Stay safe, stay together.' She gave Harry's hand a squeeze. 'You go find your mum.'

Deepika bent to give Ana a hug. It lasted a long time.

Then they headed off into the night. Again. Just the two of them. Again. They hiked up the hill in silence, feet steady on the rolling track. They curved slowly down the side of a ridge. They walked and walked, downhill, across the granite, into the valley, then along a winding plain. Past the tall, proud grass trees, their shadows eerie in the night. Past Waugal after Waugal. For what seemed like hour after hour.

'Hey, Harry,' Deepika said. 'What sort of roo can

jump higher than a house?'

But Harry wasn't listening. He'd heard something else.

They ran then, though it wasn't all that responsible. At least they both had torches now.

And it was lucky too, about the torches, because when they ran around the next corner, they saw the figure seconds before they almost ran right into her. Behind her were a couple of people in SES search-and-rescue orange, but Harry didn't care. He threw himself into Mum's arms, pack and all.

'Mum!'

'Harry!'

The two of them stood like that for a long time, a sort of strange and precarious two-headed camel. But one that made Harry's heart leap.

'I came as soon as I could,' Mum said, not letting Harry go. 'Are you okay? I've been so worried, I didn't want to go, but someone had to. That poor hiker was nearly dead. I was so worried about you, Harry.'

Harry hugged his mum hard.

'I'm so sorry, Harry,' she said. 'This is all my fault, me and that stupid phone.'

Harry shook his head, still hugged tight against Mum. 'It's my fault too,' he said. And he filled her in on everything, how they'd gone too far ahead, missed the Waugal, found the hut, then found Deepika's mum.

Mum groaned. 'Poor Ana. I can't believe this has happened.'

'She's okay,' Deepika said. 'She says she's hoping to get some good photos.'

Mum laughed then, and soon they were all laughing, a strange, relieved crazy kind of laughing, and it felt so good to laugh. Tears tickled Harry's cheeks, which made him laugh even more.

'Good photos,' Mum said, wiping her eyes. 'I've got a few of those to show you. But first, we better rescue Ana, don't you think?'

CAR PARK

A while later they were all in the car park, sipping hot chocolate from paper mugs. It was like rush hour in the clearing. There were five cars now: Deepika's, two SES utes, an ambulance, plus Alistair's dusty red sedan. And a whole bunch of extra people, including the SES volunteers who had carried Ana on a stretcher all the way to the car park.

Now paramedics were looking after Ana in the back of their ambulance.

"Looks like you'll be out of action for a month or two," said the tall one.

Ana smiled a brave smile. 'I'll be okay. I've got someone to take care of me.' She winked at Deepika.

Harry and Deepika had checked out fine, just a couple of blisters and some scrapes. Nothing a roast dinner wouldn't fix. Harry was already planning his, plus approximately four courses of dessert, and a long sleep in his own soft bed …

Ana grimaced as the paramedics braced her leg, ready for the bumpy drive out to the main road. 'How's Alistair?' she asked Mum. 'You're a real hero!'

'Not really.' Mum looked embarrassed. 'But they said he should be fine, thank goodness. They took him in the first ambulance. I guess it'll be a while before he goes hiking without water again.

Harry remembered the celebrity and the stolen diamonds. The massive cash reward could've been fun, but perhaps he'd discovered something even better. He smiled up at Mum.

'Did you get a photo with Alistair?' Ana asked. 'Do you want one with the ambulance?'

Harry's smile froze on his face. He was happy everything had turned out okay, happy everyone was safe. But the adventure was over. Mum would go right back to her phone and her emails and her messages. Nothing was surer. It had been fun to have her there for a while, really there. Well, the bits when he hadn't been totally freaking out had been fun.

But Mum shook her head. 'I'm just pleased we're all okay,' she said, hugging Harry.

Ana grimaced again as the paramedics finished up. 'I guess this kind of ruined it for everyone, hey? Have we put you off hiking forever?'

'Oh, I don't know,' said Mum. 'I hear my name's already in the logbook, at the hut. Doesn't seem right to have my name in the logbook if I've never actually been. We might have to finish the trip properly, once your leg is all fixed up.' And she kissed the top of Harry's head.

Harry nearly fell over.

Deepika climbed inside the ambulance, and he waved to her as the doors swung shut. 'See you at the hospital!'

'See you then,' she called back. 'It's going to be amazing, they have these incredible beds that go up and down by remote control, and they bring in whole trays of food, on this double-decker trolley …'

It seemed extra-quiet after the doors shut. Harry wondered if he missed her already.

MARSHMALLOW STICKS

A few months later and they were all sitting at the
wooden picnic table, out the front of the hut. Ana
had been in a cast for six weeks, and it'd taken
loads of stretching and exercise to get her leg back
to normal. But as soon as Ana was better they'd
tried the track again, and it'd all been worth it,
Harry reckoned.

'Isn't it gorgeous,' Mum sighed, looking out
across the view. 'No wonder they make huts with
only three sides.'

Ana looked up from where she was busy sorting
the dinner. Harry and Deepika had helped carry in

all the ingredients. 'Not bad, hey?'

They'd set up their sleeping bags on the raised plywood platforms. They'd brought mini mattresses too, this time. Way less barbaric, and easy to strap onto the outside of their packs.

Harry and Deepika were on one side, Mum and Ana were on the other. And Ana had brought enough warm jumpers to carpet the whole hut. Or it seemed that way to Harry.

They filled out the logbook and then, an hour or so before sunset, he and Deepika set off. It probably wouldn't take long, but you could never be sure with marshmallow sticks. Harry was hoping for two prongs.

And a couple of hours after that, following a steaming meal of creamy pasta with salami and broccoli, they were sitting around the camp fire, sorting marshmallows into pinks and whites.

Then a twig snapped.

Mum jumped. 'What was that?'

Beyond the firelight there was a thump, then another, coming closer and closer. 'Just a friendly nocturnal visitor,' Harry grinned.

They stayed around the camp fire, watching for shooting stars and trying for the perfect marshmallow, and Harry sat shoulder to shoulder with his mum. She was laughing and talking and he could see the life in her eyes, the way her smile danced with the warmth of the fire. She was looking around, really seeing. Something had happened.

She caught him staring and grinned. 'What are you thinking, mister?'

'You want me to toast you a marshmallow?' he said, sticking one on each prong of his most excellent toasting stick.

'I'd love that,' she said. And he felt her eyes follow him as he walked across to the flickering fire.

He held the marshmallows low and steady

across the glowing bed of coals. Above him the stars were bright, and behind him the trees were silhouetted against the night. It would've made an amazing photo.

But Mum kept her eyes right on him.

THE END

ABOUT CRISTY BURNE

Cristy Burne grew up climbing trees, jumping drains, chasing runaway cows and inventing stories. She is a children's author and science writer with degrees in biotechnology and science communication. She has also worked as a science circus performer, garbage analyst, and atom-smashing reporter.

For more about Cristy, go to cristyburne.com
To write to Cristy, email her at cj@cristyburne.com

ALSO BY CRISTY BURNE

Isaac arrives on the island hoping for an awesome holiday adventure, but his mum just wants him to stay safe.

Then Isaac meets Emmy. She's allowed to do whatever she wants — and she wants to have fun!

With Emmy by his side, Isaac grows more and more daring, until finally things go too far …

AVAILABLE NOW

FROM FREMANTLE PRESS

AND ALL GOOD BOOKSHOPS

First published in 2018 by
FREMANTLE PRESS
25 Quarry Street, Fremantle, Western Australia 6160
www.fremantlepress.com.au

Printed by McPherson's Printing, Australia.

    Off the track / Cristy Burne.
    ISBN 9781925591743

 A catalogue record for this
book is available from the
National Library of Australia

Fremantle Press is supported by the State Government
through the Department of Local Government, Sport and
Cultural Industries.

 Department of
**Local Government, Sport
and Cultural Industries**